Festus & Mercury

Wishing to Go Fishing

by Sven Nordqvist

Carolrhoda Books, Inc./Minneapolis

Fall had come. Festus sat at his kitchen table staring outside. The skies were an icy gray, and everything else was brown, brown, brown. The old man was not happy, not one bit.

His cat, Mercury, on the other hand, was full of beans. Up he whizzed into the chair, onto the table, and into the coffee cup— a sugar lump danced in the air and then was juggled from here to there, up and around, over and down.

"Sit still!" hissed Festus. Then he groaned, "Bah, what a day. I don't feel like doing anything."

"Great!" Mercury said merrily. "Then we can play all day."

"Oh, no," Festus said. "You'll have to play by yourself—and preferably someplace else."

"Play by myself and someplace else?" Mercury exclaimed. "I certainly do not want to do that. I want to play with you. Right here and right now. I know, we can play the cat and the acrobat, and you can be the cat!"

The old man acted like he hadn't heard a thing. He just kept looking at the dull outdoors. Drip, drip, drip. "I should go out and cut some wood," Festus muttered to himself. "Or dig up the potato patch. But it's cold out there, and all I want to do is sit."

Mercury had had about enough of the old man's bad mood. "Why feel sorry for yourself, Festus," cried Mercury, "when you've got me?!"

The cat took a bow and then stamped on a teaspoon stuck under a plate. The plate flipped up on its edge and came clattering down.

Mercury tried again. If he could bend the spoon just right, the plate would hit the coffee cup with a tangy ding. It was no easy trick. If he did it wrong, it was all clatter and no ding.

At each clatter, Festus's eyebrows pinched closer together. After only five clatters and one ding, the old man bellowed, **"STOP IT!"**

Mercury stopped in midbend, and the plate fell with a thump.

"I can't stand the noise," roared Festus. "Give me some peace and quiet. If you want to be here, sit properly on the chair, drink your coffee, and behave yourself!"

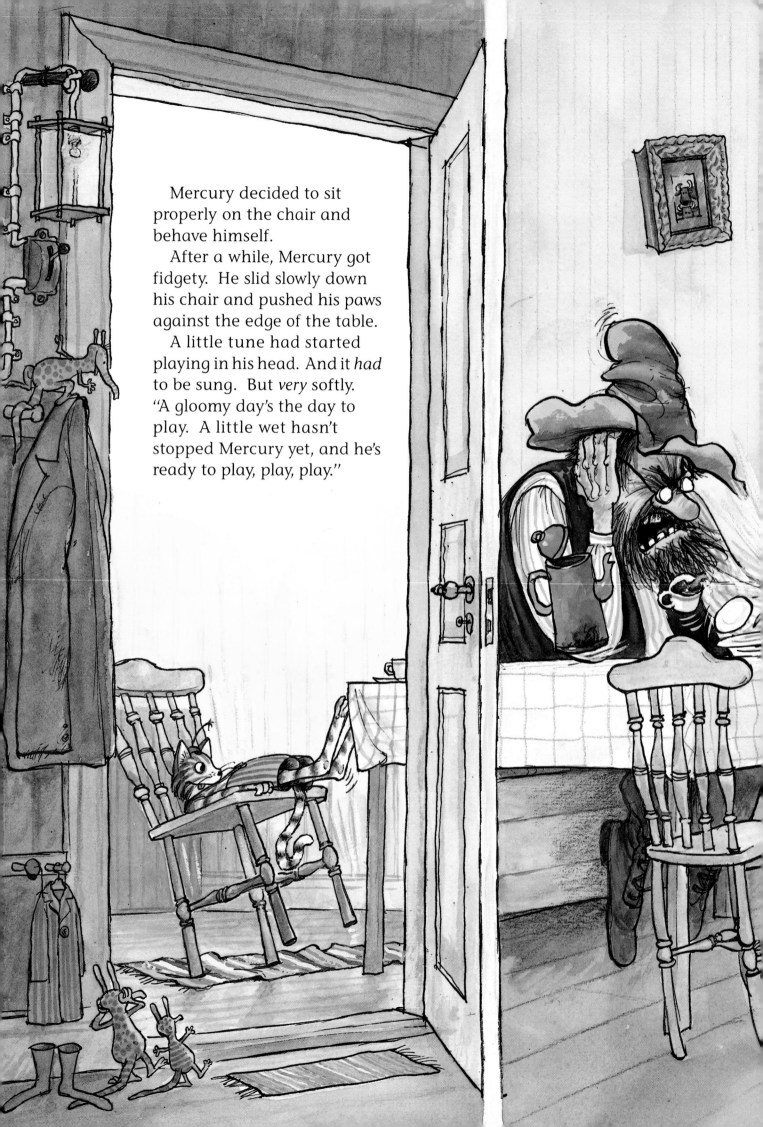

Mercury decided to sit properly on the chair and behave himself.

After a while, Mercury got fidgety. He slid slowly down his chair and pushed his paws against the edge of the table.

A little tune had started playing in his head. And it *had* to be sung. But *very* softly. "A gloomy day's the day to play. A little wet hasn't stopped Mercury yet, and he's ready to play, play, play."

Mercury sang the song as softly as he could, pushing himself back and forth from the table in time to the tune. Each time, he got a little louder and braver until . . .

"THAT'S ENOUGH!" Festus pounded the table with his fist and shouted so hard his beard flapped and . . .

CRASH! The chair flipped over, and the cat did a backward somersault, rolling on top of an empty bucket that clinked, clanked, and rattled across the floor.

"CONFOUNDED CAT!" the old man trumpeted, **"IF YOU'RE GOING TO STAY AROUND HERE, YOU HAVE TO GO OUTSIDE! I DON'T WANT TO HEAR ALL THIS RACKET. NO SINGING, NO BABBLING—NOTHING! I'M IN A BAD MOOD AND I WANT TO BE LEFT IN PEACE!"**

Mercury stared at him. He had never seen the old man so angry.
Festus sighed so deeply that he crumpled up on the kitchen bench like
a punctured car tire. "I'm sorry, Mercury," Festus said, sounding miserably
unhappy. "You shouldn't scream at your cat like that, I know. But today is
one of those days that should just disappear as fast and quietly as possible."
The old man sighed again and settled in to watch the rain.

Poor old man, thought Mercury. I'm going to have to think of something to cheer him up.

As silently as a cat, Mercury snuck up onto the kitchen table. He stood next to Festus with a claw in the air. This meant, I'm going to say just one more thing.

"Yes, what is it then?" mumbled Festus.

"We could go fishing," the cat whispered in his ear. "That would make you feel better."

"Naw," Festus moaned. "It's cold and wet, and we wouldn't catch any fish. I'm not moving an inch before this evening. Then I'll go to bed."

Good grief, thought Mercury, and he sighed almost as deeply as the old man. If only he'd go fishing, Mercury decided, then he'd be back to his old self. Maybe I can nag him just a bit . . . if I do it quietly.

Mercury hopped down from the table and opened the cupboard. Out went all the pots and pans. He wanted that fish pan at the very back. Yes, indeed, it was perfect. Then the cat fetched two wooden spoons. With his gear assembled, Mercury rowed to the very center of the floor and started to fish.

It did not take long before he got a bite. "A striped pike!" he cheered lightly. "Small but perky."

Mercury peeked up at Festus. The old man was still looking out the window.

There, another nibble. Mercury set the hook and reeled in another fish. Then another. Each time, he whispered, "Wow, I've got a bite again," and each time, he'd sneak another peek at Festus. But the old man wasn't watching. He just carried on, looking out the window.

Then Mercury hit the jackpot—a giant muskie! The cat struggled and puffed and panted and pulled and glanced secretly at Festus.

Finally, Festus snuck a one-eyed look back. But he didn't move. He just muttered, "I don't want to go fishing." Then he turned his one eye back to the window.

"You're wetter than a fish yourself," mumbled Mercury to himself. "But I've made up my mind."

The cat ran out to the toolshed and rummaged through a pile of important things until he found what he was looking for—an old fish stuck on a piece of wood. Beneath the fish was a little plaque that read: *FAT SUNFISH. Caught by Festus, 1933.* It was, of course, the fattest sunfish Festus had ever caught. Mercury tied a long piece of string to the wood and packed it in a suitcase.

Like a spy, Mercury silently slid the suitcase into the kitchen and under the table. He eased the suitcase open, grabbed the string, and jumped onto the table.

For quite a long time, Festus tried to pretend that he didn't notice the cat holding a string in the air and staring him in the eyes. At last, the old man couldn't concentrate on his sulking any longer. "What is it now?" he moaned.

Mercury held out the string to him and said softly, "Surprise!"

Festus looked at him strangely and took hold of the line.

"Look, you've got a bite!" cried the cat. "Better reel it in quick!"

Festus did as he was told. As the fat, stuffed sunfish flopped onto the table, Festus smiled a little around the corners of his mouth, but the rest of him looked as glum as before.

"I don't want to go fishing," Festus pouted and dropped the line.

You *do too*, you old coot, Mercury thought. The cat jumped off the table and was out the door without a word.

Mercury went out to the woodshed to look at the fishing rod on the wall. He pondered a while. Through a crack in the door, he could see Festus still sitting in the kitchen, staring out the window. So Mercury scrambled up the woodpile and stuck his foot under a chunk of wood.

"HELP!" he yelled. **"FESTUS, HELP! I'M STUCK!"**

When he saw Festus hurry out the door, the cat leaned back, kicking and screaming. "AHHHHH!"

"What's happened?" cried Festus, out of breath. "Have you hurt yourself?"

"I got my foot stuck," whined Mercury. "Help me get it out."

"What were you doing out here?" Festus asked, helping the cat to his feet.

"I was trying to get the fishing rod down so I could go fishing," Mercury said huffily. "Then the wood fell down on top of my foot. Can you get me the rod?"

"Mercury," said Festus, sounding tired, "you can't carry this long fishing rod all the way to the lake."

"Yes, I can. I'm certainly able to manage by myself if no one else is going to come with me," Mercury said, limping out of the shed. "Just give me the rod, and you'll see. I'll go to the lake and catch at least ten perch."

Festus shrugged and gave him the rod. Mercury started out down the hill, but the rod swayed up and down so much it set his arms to wobbling—then his legs, head, and tail. Festus couldn't help but laugh at the wiggling, jiggling, waddling little cat. "Well, now, Mercury, you can't make it the whole way down to the lake with that big rod. And with a hurt foot on top of it. I guess I'll have to come fishing too."

Festus sighed, but not as deeply as before, and he turned to fetch his backpack and rubber boots. Mercury jumped in the air with glee. But quietly. And only once. Then the cat followed the old man back to the garden to dig some worms from the potato patch.

With worms in a can, his fishing rod over his shoulder, and Mercury in his backpack, Festus started off toward the lake.

It was absolutely still and quiet. Though it had stopped raining, the air lay damp and chilly. But fresh. It felt good to get moving, Festus thought, to be out of the house and on your way somewhere, instead of just sitting there feeling how gloomy everything is.

The old man and the cat crossed the field and followed the path down to the lake. It took only a very little while before Festus had completely forgotten whatever it was that had been bothering him. In fact, he forgot that he had been bothered at all.

When Festus pushed out the boat and started to row, Mercury clambered right to the front to look out for pike. The cat had heard that northern pike could be really feisty if they were big. Of course, he wasn't afraid of them—he was not afraid of anything. But big pike scared him the very least, *if* they kept their distance.

Mercury was so excited to be out fishing with good old Festus that he couldn't keep quiet a bit longer. "Imagine if we catch a pike as big as this and it jumps on you and starts to bite you. I'll get a hold of it like this and wrestle it to the floor and ..."

Mercury jumped up and down on the edge of the boat, boxing at shadows. Just as he was about to fall overboard, Festus grabbed him.

"Sit still in the boat, cat," Festus commanded sternly. Then the old man whispered, "Do you hear how quiet it is here? Sometimes it's nice to listen to the silence."

It suddenly dawned on Mercury that he had best be quiet if he didn't want to spoil everything. But the cat couldn't help smiling. Festus was well on the way to a good mood.

The old man and the cat sat in complete silence for a whole quarter of an hour. The only sound was water lapping against the boat every now and again. The lake was silver gray, circled by the dark edges of the forest. Red and gold leaves had fallen to the ground, and everything else was a shade of brown-green-gray. But the crisp, wet air gave the colors a sharpness, a deepness, and a shine. Festus thought it all was beautiful, even better than the brash colors of summer.

"It wasn't a bad idea to go fishing," Festus said, breaking the silence.

"I definitely thought as much," said Mercury.

Just then, Festus got a nibble. Then a bite. A *real* bite.

He quickly reeled in his line and found a big sunfish at the end of it. Well, that got him going, laughing and talking. The old man was now in a good mood, for sure. The two stayed fishing for a good while longer until they both had caught a sunfish apiece.

On their way home, Mercury stated, "After we've had dinner and you've chopped the wood, we can play."

Festus started to look a bit glum again. "But I was supposed to dig up the potato patch too."

"Well," said Mercury, considering this, "you can do half. Then we'll play."

"But what about your foot?" asked the old man.

"Oh, it's fine," Mercury said, grinning. "I never really hurt it. I just used it to trick you, so you would get up off that bench."

"You little rascal!" Festus chuckled. "I suppose you'll get me to play with you too, even if I don't want to."

"Of course, you'll *want* to, Festus," said Mercury. "Just rely on me."

Library of Congress Cataloging-in-Publication Data

Nordqvist, Sven.
[Stackars Pettson. English]
Festus & Mercury : Wishing to Go Fishing / by Sven Nordqvist.
p.   cm.
Translation of: Stackars Pettson.
Summary: Mercury the cat tries to cheer up his grouchy old master
Festus through elaborate plans to get him to go fishing.
ISBN 0-87614-658-2
[1. Cats—Fiction. 2. Fishing—Fiction.] I. Title. II. Title:
Festus and Mercury: Wishing to Go Fishing.
PZ7.N7756Fd   1991
[E]—dc20   91-3147
                                                  CIP
                                                   AC

Manufactured in the United States of America

1 2 3 4 5 6 7 8 9 10 00 99 98 97 96 95 94 93 92 91